WIGGLESBOTTOM PRIMARY
THE TOILET GHOST

PAMELA BUTCHART

BECKA MOOR

nosy crow

WELCOME TO WIGGLESBOTTOM PRIMARY!

MISS RILEY

HANA

LAUREN

JAYDEN

IRFAN

EVIE

MEGAN

MILES

SUSIE

MR HARRIS

SUNITA

ROZ

GAVIN

JOEL

ANNE-MARIE

THEO

BOBBY

First published in 2015 by Nosy Crow Ltd
The Crow's Nest, 10a Lant Street
London SE1 1QR

www.nosycrow.com

ISBN: 978 0 85763 426 9

Nosy Crow and associated logos are trademarks and/or registered
trademarks of Nosy Crow Ltd

A CIP catalogue record for this book is available from the British Library.

Printed and bound in the UK by Bell and Bain Ltd, Glasgow.

Papers used by Nosy Crow are made from wood grown in
sustainable forests.

1 3 5 7 9 8 6 4 2

CONTENTS

THE TOILET GHOST

3

THE STINKY SHOE OF FORTUNE

29

THE CURSE OF THE ITCHY CARPET

63

THE TOILET GHOST

One time Gavin Ross asked to go to the toilet, and when he came back he was completely **SOAKED**.

That's when Miss Riley said, "What on **EARTH** happened to you, Gavin?"

And Gavin said, "Um. I don't know. I was just washing my hands, and then ...

IT HAPPENED."

So Gavin got sent to the nurse to get changed, and when he came back he was wearing the spare "I-had-an-accident" clothes, and he wouldn't speak to **ANYONE**. We all thought the reason Gavin wouldn't speak to anyone was because the spare trousers were too short.

But then Theo Burke put his hand up and asked if he could go to the toilet and Gavin gasped!

That's when Gavin told us he thought the boys' toilets were **HAUNTED**. Because both taps had come on **FULL BLAST** even though he barely **TOUCHED** them!

But then Miss Riley came over and told us to stop chatting and to go back to our own tables. And then she tried to give the Toilet Pass to Theo Burke, but he said he didn't need to go any more, even though we all knew he did.

At break-time, we all ran outside and sat in the long grass. Sunita Ram said that we should all put our coats around Gavin's shoulders and take good care of him, because of the Toilet Ghost, so we did.

Sunita said that Gavin must be feeling very weak and tired because of the shock he had had, and Gavin nodded that he was. Then he pulled his knees up and started rocking a bit. So I took my Ribena out of my pocket and tried to give it to Gavin, for energy.

But then Susie Keys screamed,

"NO! DON'T DRINK IT!"

And that's when Susie explained that none of the boys could drink any juice **OR** water, because then they'd need to go to the toilet and the Toilet Ghost would

GET THEM.

So we all ran around the playground telling the boys in our class about the Toilet Ghost and the **JUICE BAN**.

But then at lunch all the boys got **REALLY** thirsty because it was Chicken Curry day and everyone had Spicy Mouth.

So Sunita Ram said that Gavin and the other boys should just sip a **TINY** bit of water each. And then she filled a glass and passed it around our table. Gavin Ross just took a tiny sip, and so did Jayden King, but when it was Irfan Baxter's turn he gulped down the **WHOLE GLASS**!

And everyone was shocked. But then Irfan Baxter said that he couldn't help it, and that he was just **TOO THIRSTY**. And then he poured himself **ANOTHER** glass of water and drank that one too!

Everyone was really worried about Irfan, because we all knew he would need to go to the toilet soon, and that the Toilet Ghost was going to get him.

After lunch, Irfan Baxter couldn't even play football, which he **ALWAYS** does. He just had to sit in the long grass and keep his legs crossed really tight and listen to Gavin Ross tell us all about the Toilet Ghost again.

Then, just before the bell went, Irfan said, "**I'M GOING TO BURST!**"

And he started running towards the boys' toilets, so we all ran after him.

When we got there, Irfan ran inside and Susie Keys told everyone to cross their fingers, so we did.

But then there was a loud rattling sound from inside the toilet and everyone started screaming,

"THE TOILET GHOST!"

And Irfan Baxter came running out, and he looked like he was going to wee himself **ANY SECOND**. And that's when Susie Keys shouted, "You're going to have to use the girls' toilets!"

But all the boys shouted,

"NO WAY!"

Except for Irfan, who just pushed past us and ran straight into the **GIRLS' TOILETS**! And everyone **GASPED**.

Then Theo Burke and some of the other boys started jumping around and saying that they were going to burst too. And then they **ALL** ran into the girls' toilets!

And that's when the Deputy Head, Mr Harris, turned up, and he said, "What's all the screaming about?!"

So we told him that it was because of the Toilet Ghost that lived in the boys' toilets. And then we told him that all the boys were in the girls' toilets, and that made him really cross. Mr Harris knocked on the door and told all the boys to come out **RIGHT AWAY**.

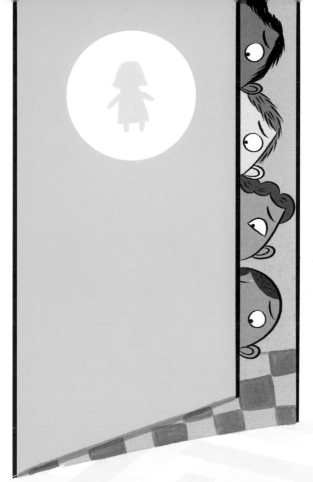

Then he said he was going to check what was going on in the boys' toilets, even though we told him not to and that the Toilet Ghost would definitely **GET HIM**.

But Mr Harris didn't listen to us. He just opened the door and went in, even though we could still hear the rattling noise.

And then Mr Harris shouted, "Everything's fine in here. You're just being silly. There's no such thing as a Toilet— **AAAAARRRRRGGGGHHHHH!**"

And then the rattling noise turned into a **SCREECHING NOISE** and Mr Harris **SQUEALED** and came running out of the boys' toilets, even faster than Irfan Baxter had! And he was **COMPLETELY SOAKED**! He definitely looked like he'd seen a Toilet Ghost!

Mr Harris ran right past us, so we all ran after him, and that's when Miss Riley came out of the staff room and told everyone to stop running and took us back to our classroom.

Miss Riley tried to calm us down, but we couldn't stop thinking about the Toilet Ghost, and Gavin Ross was still rocking a bit.

But then Mr Harris turned up wearing shorts and a T-shirt from the "I-had-an-accident" box. And he

still had his shoes and socks on.

Everyone had to cover their mouths to stop themselves from laughing and getting told off.

And then Mr Harris said, "The caretaker says some of the pipes in the boys' toilet have burst. Obviously."

And I had to bite the inside of my cheek to stop myself laughing out loud because Mr Harris' shorts were **SO** small and they were **COVERED** in flowers!

And then Mr Harris said the boys were to use the staff toilets

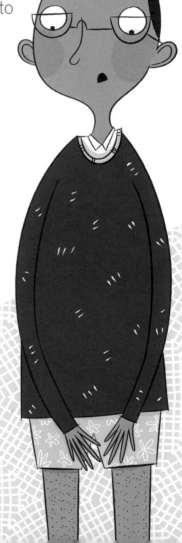

next door to our classroom until the plumbing was fixed, and that there were definitely **NO** Toilet Ghosts in there.

As soon as Mr Harris left, everyone **BURST** out laughing and Miss Riley laughed so much tears came out!

But then we heard a scream coming from the staff toilet next door. And then Mrs McClusky rushed past our classroom and she was **SOAKED**!

And that's when we knew the Toilet Ghost **WAS** real and that it had **STRUCK AGAIN**!

THE STINKY SHOE OF FORTUNE

When we did our class Talent Show, Joel Jack **AND** Miles McKay said that they were going to do a

MAGIC ACT.

Joel Jack stood up first and showed us all a packet of cheese and onion crisps. Then he asked for a volunteer from the audience to eat one to prove that they were **REAL CRISPS**.

EVERYONE put their

hands up, but Joel Jack picked Miss Riley (even though she didn't have her hand up) and then she ate one and said, "Yes. They're real."

Joel Jack said that he was going to do the

"AMAZING VANISHING CRISPS ACT"

and then he put a big towel over his head. And then there was lots of crunching.

We all **KNEW** that Joel Jack was just **EATING** the crisps to make them **VANISH**, because we could **HEAR HIM**.

Then Joel Jack said, "Could a volunteer from the audience please pass me a bag of salt and vinegar?"

But Miss Riley said **NO**, and that it was time for a new act. So that's when Miles McKay stood up, took off his **LEFT SHOE** and held it up in the air.

Miss Riley told Miles to put his shoe back on, and to get on with his act. But Miles said that his shoe **WAS** his act and that it was a **MAGIC** shoe that could **PREDICT THE FUTURE**. And then he started **WAVING** it at everyone.

Lauren Carr said that the shoe was **STINKING**, but Miles said, "If you can smell **THE SHOE** it means that **THE SHOE** wants to tell you something."

So Miles held **THE SHOE** over Lauren's head, and Lauren held her nose, and then **THE SHOE** started **SHAKING**.

Then Miles said, "**THE SHOE** says you will have a cheese and jam sandwich for your lunch today!"

So Lauren took her sandwich out of her lunchbox, and opened it up. And then she **GASPED** because it **WAS** a cheese and jam sandwich, and she held it up for everyone to see. And we were all **SHOCKED**!

Then **EVERYONE** started shouting,

"DO ME NEXT! DO ME!"

But Miles said, "**THE SHOE** goes where **THE SHOE** goes." And then he held it over Irfan Baxter's head and said, "You will play football today. You will score one goal. Maybe more."

And that made Irfan Baxter smile **A LOT** because he

LOVES football.

Then Miles held **THE SHOE** over Miss Riley's head and said, "Today you will get a **BIG SURPRISE!**"

And Miss Riley said, "Oooh! How lovely!"

I was **DESPERATE** for it to be my turn, but then the bell rang, and Miles had to put **THE SHOE** back on so we could all go for lunch.

EVERYONE was talking about **THE SHOE** at lunch. Lauren Carr even said that she was going to keep half of her sandwich as **EVIDENCE** that **THE SHOE** had **POWERS**.

Then Irfan Baxter said that he was going to play football, so everyone ran outside to watch, and Miles waved **THE SHOE** at him.

When Irfan scored his first goal everyone went **MAD** and the boys even picked Miles up off the ground and chanted,

"SHOE, SHOE, SHOE, SHOE!"

That afternoon, Lauren Carr started crying because she couldn't find her break-time snack in her tray. So Miles held **THE SHOE** up to his ear and nodded as if **THE SHOE** was whispering to him, and then he said, "**THE SHOE** has a riddle for you. What is yellow and blue and not made of poo?"

So we all looked around for something that was yellow and blue and not made of poo, and that's when I saw the **BIG BEANBAG** so I shouted, "The beanbag!" and everyone rushed over. And when we picked it up we found Lauren's KitKat underneath!

So Lauren gave Miles half of her KitKat to say thanks.

Then Miss Riley started **SCREAMING** that there was a **RAT** in her handbag! And then she shut herself in the cupboard.

So we all looked and saw a **RAT'S TAIL** sticking out of her bag!

Then the Deputy Head, Mr Harris, came rushing in and asked us what was going on, so we told him and he said, "**STAND BACK**." And then he used a ruler to flip the rat's tail into the bag so it didn't get squished, then he closed the bag really quickly.

Then he told Miss Riley that the situation was

"UNDER CONTROL,"

and that she could come out now. But she wouldn't.

That's when I remembered what Miles had said earlier, about Miss Riley's

BIG SURPRISE,

and I realised that Miles hadn't said that it was going to be a **GOOD** surprise.

So I shouted through the door to Miss Riley that the rat must have been her

BIG SURPRISE,

just like Miles had said. And as soon as I said that she opened the door and said, "Miles McKay! Did you put a **RAT** in my handbag?!"

And Miles said no.

But then Mr Harris said, "Miles. Did you put a rat in Miss Riley's bag?"

And Miles said yes. But then he said that it wasn't a **REAL** rat, and that it was only made of **RUBBER**, and that it was all part of his **ACT**. Then Miles explained that **THE SHOE DIDN'T** have powers and that he had just **TRICKED US**!

Miles said that he'd peeked inside Lauren's packed-lunch box that morning to see her sandwich, and that he'd taken her KitKat and hidden it under the **BIG BEANBAG**. And also that he'd put the rat in Miss Riley's bag when she wasn't looking.

But then Irfan Baxter said, "If it was a trick, how did you know I was going to play football and score a goal?"

And Miles said that Irfan

ALWAYS

plays football at lunch and that he

ALWAYS

scores a goal, and that he probably would
have scored even

MORE

goals if everyone hadn't stopped playing to
chant "**SHOE! SHOE!**"

So then Lauren Carr **DEMANDED** half her KitKat back. And Miles got told off by Miss Riley **AND** by Mr Harris for going through other people's **BELONGINGS** and for giving Miss Riley a terrible fright.

I felt sorry for Miles, because he'd only been trying to do a good trick, and he'd even told us how he'd done it, and the magicians that I've seen have **NEVER** told me how they do their tricks, not even when I've asked **ALL** the way through their act.

So after break, I sneaked under our table when no one was looking and put **LOADS** of glue all over Miles' left shoe. And then I sprinkled a whole tube of green glitter over it!

When Miles saw his shoe, he was **SHOCKED**!

"How did **THAT** happen?!" he said.

And so I said, "Only **THE SHOE** knows, Miles. Only **THE SHOE** knows."

THE CURSE OF THE ITCHY CARPET

Last week when we were doing Show and Tell, Bobby Henderson brought in a shoe box that had **DANGER** and **DO NOT OPEN** and **BEWARE** written all over it.

We all thought that Bobby had brought his pet hamster, The Warrior, to school again. And so did Miss Riley because she said, "Bobby! Have you brought your hamster to school again?!"

Because we are

NOT ALLOWED

to bring anything that is **ALIVE** to Show and Tell, not even our pets, or a tiny fly.

But Bobby said that he hadn't, and that The Warrior was at home in his cage.

Then Bobby said, "What is in this box is **DEFINITELY** not a pet." And he held the box up over his head when he said it. And his eyes went really wide.

Then Bobby started going right up to people's faces and saying stuff like, "You can **LOOK** but you can't **TOUCH**," and "You won't **BELIEVE** what's in here," and, "The Queen will **DEFINITELY** want to know about this!"

I had **NO IDEA** what was in the box, but I knew then that it couldn't be Bobby's hamster because I didn't think the Queen would really be that interested in someone else's hamster when she probably has loads of her own hamsters at the palace anyway.

Then Bobby said that what was in the box was an **ANCIENT CURSE** and that he'd found it in the playground, behind the Big Bush.

Everyone **GASPED** when he said it, and Susie Keys put her coat on and said that she was going home, because that's what Susie Keys **ALWAYS** does when she doesn't like something.

But then Miss Riley told Susie to take her coat off, and said that there **DEFINITELY WEREN'T** any **ANCIENT CURSES** in the school, and that curses didn't exist, and that Bobby was just being silly.

So then Sunita Ram said that Bobby was telling **LIES** and that the box was probably empty.

So Bobby **DARED** Sunita to open the box.

But Miss Riley said, "OK, that's enough. It's time to put the box away. Give it to me."

But before Bobby had a chance to give Miss Riley the box, Sunita Ram grabbed it and pulled the lid right off, and everyone started **SCREAMING**, because we all thought that Sunita Ram had just let an ancient curse loose in our classroom!

Everyone started running around and pulling their jumpers over their heads and Miss Riley kept yelling, "**CALM DOWN!**" but nobody would and loads of people ran into the store cupboard and shut the door, and Bobby hid under Miss Riley's desk, and even Sunita Ram was covering her ears so the curse couldn't get her.

Then the Deputy Head came in because of all the screaming, and told us all to sit down **AT ONCE**, so we did, because he said it in his **SERIOUS VOICE**.

Then Miss Riley whispered something in his ear. And we all thought that it was about the **ANCIENT CURSE**, because he ran out of the classroom right away.

But then he came back with Susie Keys, and we realised that he'd just gone to get Susie before she ran all the way home.

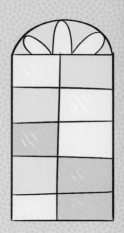

Then Miss Riley said that there was **NO REASON** to be worried, and told us that the box was empty, and promised us that there were no such things as **ANCIENT CURSES**.

Then Miss Riley said it was time for our story. So we all sat down in the story corner and listened as Miss Riley read us our book. And I had started to forget all about the **ANCIENT CURSE** because nothing bad had happened, and Miss Riley had promised it wasn't real and also because the story was about two dogs.

But then I noticed that Susie Keys was scratching her head

LOADS.

And so was Joel Jack.

And then Megan McNally put
her hand up and said, "Miss, my leg is itchy."

Miss Riley told Megan to stop fidgeting and then she went back to reading the story.

But then Bobby said, "I'm itchy too. It's **THE CURSE**! It's making us all **ITCH!**"

And as soon as he said that, **LOADS** of people started scratching, and all of a sudden **MY** legs felt really itchy too, and so did my arm!

But then Miss Riley got cross, because Bobby had mentioned **THE CURSE** again. And also because we were all scratching instead of listening to the story like we were supposed to.

So we all tried to pay attention, and to scratch quietly. But then Miss Riley started wriggling around on her seat while she was reading. And her voice started to go up and down in a weird way.

And then she said, "And then the dog looked at the RA-bbit and… **OUCH!!!**"

And she jumped up out of her seat and started rubbing her bottom!

And then Susie Keys yelled, "**OUCH!** My ankle! Something just **BIT ME!**"

And then Bobby shouted,

"THE CURSE!
IT'S THE CURSE!
IT'S BITING US!"

And I looked at Miss Riley and I could **TELL** that she was starting to believe us about **THE CURSE**, because her eyes had gone **REALLY** wide and she was still rubbing her bottom.

But then all of a sudden Evie Macintosh started crying, and she ran over to Miss Riley and said, "I'm so sorry, Miss Riley! They got out!"

And Miss Riley looked really confused, and then she said, "What got out, Evie? Do you mean the curse? I've already told you all, there's no such thing as ancient cur—"

And that's when Evie said,

"**NO! My ANTS,** Miss Riley. They got **OUT!**"

And we all gasped. And that's when Evie explained that she'd forgotten all about the **NO PETS RULE** for Show and Tell, and that she'd brought in her **ANT FARM**. And that she was scared that she would get told off, so she hid it under one of the tables.

Then Evie said that someone must've knocked it over by mistake when we were all running from **THE CURSE**.

And that's when Miss Riley went really weird in the face, and started scratching her bottom loads, especially when Evie said that there were at least **TEN THOUSAND ANTS** in her **ANT FARM**.

Then Miss Riley said that she had to go to the toilet, and she sent Miles next door to get the Deputy Head.

But then as soon as Miss Riley ran out, Evie Macintosh started crying because she said that the ants were her pets, and that she didn't want to lose even one of them, and that they all had names, and that they were all her favourites.

So that's when we said that we would help her find them and we crawled around the classroom on our hands and knees trying to see the ants and get them back into their farm. But it wasn't very easy because they were tiny, and they could crawl **REALLY** fast, and also because I kept accidentally squishing them with my knees.

Then Mr Harris came rushing in and he said, "What's going on **NOW**? Is it this curse nonsense again?"

And we said that it wasn't. And that it was ants.

And he looked really confused, and then he said, "Where's Miss Riley?"

And Susie Keys said, "She had to go to the bathroom. She's got ants in her pants!"

And as soon as she said that, everyone **BURST** out laughing! And we just **COULDN'T** stop!